Have You Seen My Blankie?

For my mum and Andy xx
L.R.

For Princess Harriet Gwendoline,
with love from Auntie Paula

First published 2019 by Nosy Crow Ltd,
The Crow's Nest, 14 Baden Place, Crosby Row, London SE1 1YW
www.nosycrow.com

ISBN 978 1 78800 198 4 (HB)
ISBN 978 1 78800 199 1 (PB)

A CIP catalogue record for this book is available from the British Library.

Printed in China
Papers used by Nosy Crow are made from wood grown in sustainable forests.

10 9 8 7 6 5 4 3 2 1 (HB)
10 9 8 7 6 5 4 3 2 1 (PB)

Have You Seen My Blankie?

Lucy Rowland & Paula Metcalf

Once, inside a palace,
lived a young princess called Alice,
and Alice had a blankie
that she always took to bed.

This blankie was SO cuddly!
So soft and warm and snuggly!

But one day...

...it went
missing!

"Where's my
blankie?"
Alice said.

Alice ran across the floor
and hurried to the palace door.
She called to Jack, her **brother**,
who was playing in his den.

He said, "Oh, yes, I'm certain
that I used it as a **curtain**,
but that was quite some time ago —
a **giant** took it then."

Alice tracked the giant down.
She rang his doorbell with a frown.
Giant Jim said, "Come on in!
I've made some lovely pies."

He said, "I had your blankie
and I used it as a hankie,
but then a witch discovered it
and flew off through the skies!"

Alice started out once more.
She knocked upon the witch's door.

The witch said, "Oh, your blankie? Yes, it made a lovely cloak.
But if I'm not mistaken, dear, my lovely cloak was taken!"
She pointed to the trees, where Princess Alice spied some smoke.

Alice went exploring and
she heard some noisy snoring!
She walked into the forest
and was trying to be brave . . .

But then she saw her blankie
and a dragon looking cranky.
"Who disturbs my slumbers?"
roared the dragon from his cave.

Alice felt a little scared.
"That's my blankie!" she declared.
But suddenly . . .

... she realised that this dragon
wasn't tough!

The dragon sadly bowed his head.
"It's just so very SOft," he said.
"Your blankie helps me sleep
because my bed is cold and rough."

Princess Alice looked quite cross.
"It's time to show him just who's boss!"
But when she reached for Blankie ...
Oh! The dragon looked so blue.

And Alice thought about it.
"Well, he'll never sleep without it.
I wonder," said the princess,
"if there's something I can do?"

Just then she had a good idea.
"Yes, of course! The answer's clear . . .

... We'll find you something snuggly,
soft and
warm," the princess said.

The dragon whispered, "Oh, yes please!"
He gave the blankie one last squeeze,
then handed it to Alice as he wriggled from his bed.

Alice and her new-found friend left the woods and ...

round the bend . . .
they came upon the **witch's** house.
They hoped that she could help.
The witch said, "Try my snuggly cat?
She's sleeping here inside my hat."

"But cats are far too **scratchy**!"
said the dragon with a yelp.

The dragon was now trying
to stop himself from crying . . .

So Alice spoke to Giant Jim
(who gave it quite some thought).
"My feather cushion's soft!" he said.
"Perhaps you could try that instead?"

"But feathers make me sneezy!"
said the dragon with a snort.

ATcHooO!

The dragon's tears were flowing,
so the princess kept on going.
They flew to find her **brother**.
"Do you have any ideas?"

"Socks are **warm!**" young Jack replied.
"I've got an extra pair inside."

"But socks are far too **stinky!**" said the dragon through his tears.

Princess Alice felt so bad.
The dragon looked so very sad.
He sobbed, "I need a blankie
or I'll never sleep tonight!"

Alice stroked the dragon's head
and then she very gently said,
"Don't give up! I promise we'll find
something that's just right!"

The dragon followed Alice
and they went inside the palace.

"We need something that's soft,"
she told him, "warm and snuggly too."
They tried the kitchen and the porch.
They checked the attic
(with a torch).

Then, in her bedroom, Alice cried,
"I've just the thing for you!"

With lots of noisy puffing,
some heaving and some huffing . . .

the princess showed the dragon,

"Look . . .

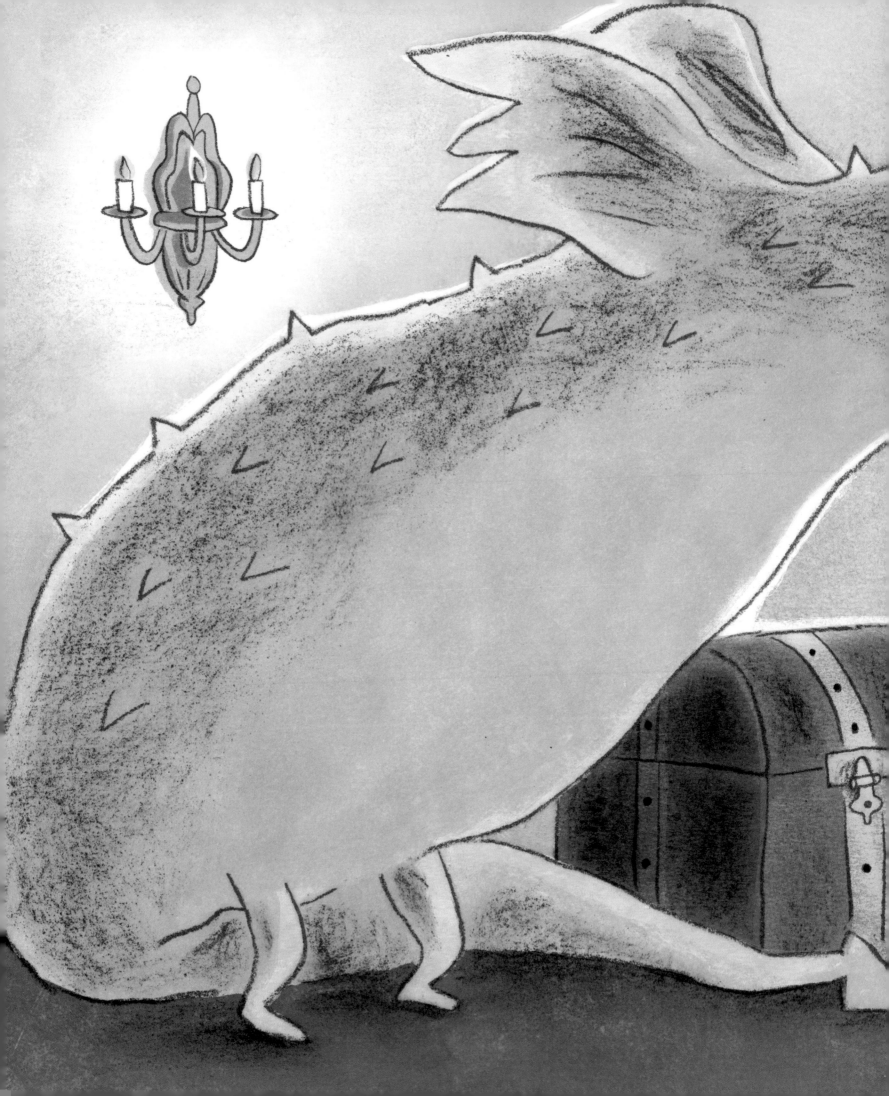

...my fluffy teddy bear!"

The dragon, beaming brightly, held on to the teddy tightly.

And Alice felt so pleased that she'd found **just** the thing to share.

Ta-daaa!

Inside a royal palace,
lives a young princess called Alice . . .
but now she has a dragon
who will often come to stay!

So, anyone who's scheming,
beware the dragon dreaming.
He's guarding Ted and Blankie . . .

. . . so you'd better keep away!